Frog

Huggums

Little Sister

Gator

Bat Child

Maurice & Molly

Oscar

Little Sister's Bracelet

by MERCER MAYER

Little Sister put on her new bracelet. She took her pail and went to play with her friends.

But she lost her bracelet
while she was playing.

"I lost my new bracelet,"
cried Little Sister.
"We will find it for you," said Max.

"Don't worry," said Skat Owl.

"I can look from
the treetops," said Max.

"I can look from
the hilltops,"
said Mooso.

"I can look from high in the sky," said Skat Owl.

Possum Child said,
"I can look
under things."

Mouse said,
"I can look inside things."

Bat Child said,
"I can search
in dark places."

Malcom sniffed around on the ground.

Bun Bun looked under the briar bushes.

Mooso looked behind
the tree.

Little Critter fished for it.

Frog and Gator swam for it.

Maurice and Molly dug for it.

They all searched high and low, but
no one could find Little Sister's bracelet.

There was just one place
where no one thought to look.

And that's where Little Sister found it.
"It was in my pail!" said Little Sister.

Possum Child

Mouse

Max

Seaweed

Little Critter

Skat Owl

Mooso

Malcom